BLONOTE

BLONOtE

I wrote these short bursts of thought
during my tenure as a late night radio DJ,
signing off with them instead of a customary
"good night."

The aphorisms here don't pretend to be
the beginning or end of any grand idea,
but I'm hoping that they can be the beginning
of an inspiration or an end to a worry.

Place this book somewhere within reach,
for those moments when your heart is restless.

6

I must leave.

Not to find my way,
but to hold myself back a moment
from continuing down the wrong one.

Fear
is Expectation with her head hung low.

7

8

What I need is a diet
that will lose me the weight of the world.

Love is like a footprint.
It's clear only after you step away.

10

I thought about giving up.
Then I chose to give up the thought.

What a
rainy day is
trying
to tell you

is that
you're not
the only one.

11

The things you're hanging on to
may become the things that hang you.

I must have a designated rain cloud.

13

Actress Gong Hyo Jin's handwriting

배우 공효진의 손글씨

They say life is like riding a bicycle.
Why does it feel like I'm the only one
that's been given a unicycle?

인생은 자전거 타는 것과
같다는데, 왜 나만
외발자전거를 타고 있는 것 같지?

16

Photography
teaches you that a second is a measure of eternity.

Before you decide that I'm nothing you expected,
could you try to expect nothing but me?

17

18

" "
.

The end of the story that is us,
dwindled and dark,
couldn't be more aptly punctuated.

It kills me
that I see nothing but you when I close my eyes,
but everything but you when I open them.

19

Lovers build castles in the sky,
only to realize they were made of sand.

Being happy
first requires you to *be*.

21

22

To die without regrets,
one must live irrevocably.

A masterpiece is created
not by the hands of an artist,
but by the hands of time.

You say you want to live life like a movie.
Keep in mind that there's a running time.

다들 영화처럼
살고 싶다고 하는데
그럼
두 시간만 살 건가

Film director Park Chan Wook's handwriting

영화감독 박찬욱의 손글씨

26

She was reading a book of poetry.
From afar, he was reading her.

Turns out, time and gravity are like-minded.

27

There's a parking lot in my heart
and too many people have left without their cars.

My place in this world
is far from somewhere I can call "my place."

29

Unattained
love
is still called
love.

Why do we
call
an unattained
dream
failure?

The Earth remains round
but we're doing everything
we can to make it flat.

Busker Busker Jang Beom June's handwriting

버스커 버스커 장범준 의 손글씨

I'm not an outsider.
I'm just not near you.

저는 아웃사이더가 아니라
당신 곁에 없는 겁니다.

34

Something that can't be seen until it can't be seen:
someone breathing.

As I try on a coat he once loved,
I realize just how warm my father was.

35

36

A hundred people were gathered in front of a painting.
Ninety-eight of them saw a circle,
and the remaining two
each saw a triangle and a square.

The two fell in love.

When things don't go your way,
they might be suggesting a better way to go.

37

38

Life is short and a season is shorter.
Relish the heat; relish the cold.

You're busy wondering whether I can or can't see the forest for the trees.

I'm busy gazing at the sky.

39

40

Pure

[noun] Not mixed with anything else.

Doesn't seem so pure to me.

When you say I've changed,
it only means you weren't willing to change with me.

41

42

I overheard two ghosts having a conversation.

"It's their world that frightens me."

You sigh, saying that it's getting harder to
follow your heart.
But you never had much of a heart to follow.

43

An angel will never see the Devil as an angel,
but to the Devil, it's the angel that is the Devil.

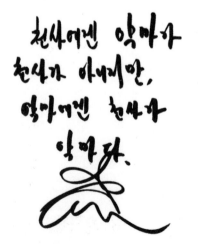

BigBang G-DRAGON's handwriting

빅뱅 권지용의 손글씨

46

The sound of thought
isn't the sound of cogs turning;
it is the sound of a pencil sharpener turning.

The problem is that my memory of you
simply happens to be photogenic.

47

48

I don't mind being strange
but I mind being a stranger.

You puzzle over whether
you should follow your head
or follow your heart.

Your head and your heart,
hand in hand all this time,
puzzle over you.

Student Do Hye Yeon's handwriting

학생 **도혜연**의 손글씨

Something that is unexplainable

is either a miracle

or

you're just not that good at explaining.

설명할수어ㄴ이ㅇ은 기적이거나
그냥 이네가 설명을 잘 못하는거야

52

I need a friend that expects
nothing of me.

It's just one letter,
N.

How is it that it changes 'ever'
completely?

The thought in my head as I jump into a new relationship:

"Is that a parachute or a backpack?"

They say time flies

but you keep breaking its wings.

56

You don't have to know the meaning of life to breathe.
You don't have to know what happiness is to smile.

Fear of death
originates from an impatience with life.

57

After you left me,
I bought my first pair of mittens.

이별 후
처음으로 장갑을 사고 있다.

Radio writing staff Kim Jae Yeon's handwriting

라디오 작가 **김재연**의 손글씨

People read voraciously once they're on a plane.

If you want someone to learn,
keep them seated if you will,
but also raise them up.

"Where do you find inspiration?"

It's inspiration that finds me.

61

62

I have a friend who has trouble throwing stuff away.
His room looks just like my heart.

If your mind is heavy, stop dragging it around.

63

64

Mistake. Mischief. Sin.

That each has its own name
means not to treat them as the same thing.

My biography
is gonna end up being one hell of a dark fairy tale.

66

I'm learning that "I need you"
is far from "I want you."

This bar table.
This
bathroom
wall.

Even without
you,
I have things
to lean on.

67

My childhood diary
is like an abandoned amusement park.

On the way up, stairs.
On the way down, a cliff.

Love.

69

Turns out,
"No pain, no gain" is right.

Look at all the pain I've gained.

Still.
It's either moving or unmoving.

I mean both when I say I love you still.

An award show was held.
One that takes back the awards given out the previous year.

The acceptance speeches were filled with excuses.

People who run the tabloids
must be yearning for a dark, starless sky.

73

My mother's job is done.

Now I'm the one trying to give birth to me.

엄마는 여전히
나를 낳기위해진통중이시다

Student Kwon Hee Jun's handwriting

학생 *권희준* 의 손글씨

They say lovers start to resemble each other.
I say, we became lovers because we resemble each other.

If you want to hear only what you want to hear,
let me hear it too.

77

A tone-deaf man singing
probably sounds pitch perfect in his own mind, right?

That's how I am when I'm around you.

The world doesn't revolve around me, I know.
The problem is that I don't want myself in it at all.

If I was a fish
inside a tank at a fish market,
I'd go out of my way
to not look fresh.

내가 시장 수조
안에 있는 물고기라면
일부러 안 싱싱한척
할 것 같아

Comedian Yang Se Hyung's handwriting

개그맨 **양세형**의 손글씨

The reason why I can't see the light
is because you have your eyes closed.

Sometimes the unimaginable
occurs in order to fatten our imagination.

How can
your heart,
so unwilling
to be moved,

move
others?

Someone up there
must be speeding up time,
just enough for no one to notice.

The object mistakenly thought to itself,

"I was put in this box
because I'm precious."

"I hope something good happens to you."

That I have you who says this to me
is that good thing.

Musician You Hee Yeol's handwriting

뮤지션 유희열의 손글씨

I loved you like I was belting out the notes.
But to you it was all a hum.

엄청나를 사랑했는데
그 사랑을 너를
흥얼거림 정도로 느꼈나보다.

No wonder money doesn't grow on trees.
It's all the way down there being the root of all evil.

Growing up
doesn't mean growing right.

I need an external hard drive
for all these emotions.

If you want to see more than just the tip of the iceberg,
get ready to dive in.

93

What we call a crush
deserves a more fitting name: crushed.

If you want
to be
recognized,

first
recognize
yourself.

95

I wish I had a clone.
Then again, I'm not doing much with the body I have.

Memories feel closer
when they're far out of reach.

98

If I could reshape my heart,
I'd turn it into a ball
and pass it around with you.

There comes an age
when what was hard becomes easy
and what was easy becomes hard.

An adult's definition of positivity:

"I only think about good things (for me)."

I've been holding on to a knot for so long
that I don't know if I was tying it
or untying it.

Advertiser Seo Yoon's handwriting

광고인 ㅅㅓ윤의 손글씨

The moment love begins to die

is when the things you want to know about each other
is exceeded by the things you want to not know about each other.

권태,
알고 싶은 것보다
모르고 싶은 것이
많아지는 때.

104

Someone placed an ashtray right next to
a No Smoking sign.
This is how you play hard to get.

In such a cold world,
why covet being *cool*?

A child smiles at a butterfly
and cringes at a moth.

The moth is confused.

Submerging yourself in a shallow thought
doesn't turn it into a deep thought.

108

When I was young,
I searched for someone who will stand by me.
Now I'm searching for someone who will stand me.

The temperature of the heart
has nothing to do with the weather.

Kkotsbom Creative director Kim Hye Jin's handwriting

꽃봄 크리에이티브 디렉터 김혜진 의손글씨

Some goodbyes
bring back all of life's goodbyes.

어떤 이별은
살아온 모든 이별을 불러온다.

112

"As good as it gets"
isn't the optimistic thought it pretends to be.

We're no longer living in an age of rags to riches.
We're living in an age of rags for riches.

Don't wait around until they miss you.
By that time,
they'll have completely missed you.

I'm not afraid. I'm not afraid. I'm not afraid.

An incantation to summon fear.

115

116

I did all that I could.
It's just that I needed to do what I couldn't.

The only thing you should pluck to make yours
is a flower.

117

118

The problem is that I've prayed "just this once..."
more than just this once.

Her boyfriend
was too much of a boy
and too little of a friend.

120

Someone deep in your heart
is also that much harder to reach.

There are people
who wait for Halloween
to take off their masks.

"How's work?"
"How's married life?"

I used to think,
none of your business.

But now,
thanks to coworkers and a spouse
who never ask how I am,

I think to myself,
thank you.

"Stop sighing."

"This is the only way I know how to breathe."

I tried so
hard
to let go of
my anger,

only to be
angry
that I let it go.

A selfish person
should learn something from loneliness.

My day to day,
as a playlist,
would be one long song on repeat.

The two hands that left me this scarf
would have given me more warmth.

On nights when work ends late,
I find myself wishing
that home would come to me.

일이 늦게 끝날 땐
집이 나에게 와줬으면
좋겠다는 생각을 한다.

Model, Actress Lee Sung Kyoung's handwriting

모델·배우 **이성경**의 손글씨

To know whether it's the entrance or the exit,
you need to open the door.

I don't have much time left
to fear that I don't have much time left.

To some,
a wedding invitation
must seem like a subpoena.

If you're going to live in my head,
pay some rent at the least.

133

134

When I'm all cried out,
thank God
that there are books, films, and songs
to do the job for me.

I want to
leave
for somewhere
I won't want
to leave.

"I've got the blues."

I misheard it as "I've got a noose,"
but that's exactly what was meant.

The only one that will stick by your side
is unfortunately stuck behind a mirror.

Maybe some things are too small
to have my heart in it.

The reason why best friends fight
is because they're used to being there for
each other after a fight.

Student Nam Su Young's handwriting

학생 남 수 영의 손글씨

The things we've let go of
find it very hard to let go of us.

우리가 놓아버린 것들이
여전히 우릴 향해 손 내밀고 있어요.

Even the heart has a peak season.
Please check before expecting accommodations.

The barrel wasn't unspoiled to begin with,
if a rotten apple was in it.

Find someone to walk with you
who will make you forget
where you were headed.

I'm not saying that you're my everything.
I'm simply saying that without you, I'd be nothing.

The frequency of getting things to go
may be an accurate measure of how adult you are.

Remember that even magicians
have mothers performing the greatest magic of all.

Some people make love
not with the body
nor with the heart
but with the passing of time.

어떤 사람은
마음도 아닌
몸도 아닌
세월처럼 하는 것

Student Kim Seo Hyun's handwriting

학생 **김서현**의 손글씨

150

Beneath thin ice,
freedom flows.

Here we are taking guarded steps in search of it.

To measure love's worthlessness
by its brevity
is to measure a life's worth
by its longevity.

We live in strange times indeed,
when we can become close with someone that is distant
and become distant with someone that was never close.

When
you treat
someone
like a set of
stairs,

you will trip
and fall.

Love is
when you want to give someone what you cherish most
but they ask for what you cherish least.

Without family, there is only you.
And without you, there is no family.

The Black Skirts Cho Hyu Il's handwriting

검정치마 조 휴 일의 손글씨

Bought a used guitar.

Never imagined that a dream abandoned
could be this cheap.

중고 악기를 샀다.
누군가의 못다 한 꿈이
이렇게 값싸다니.

158

It's a "he said, she said" situation.
The problem is that neither of them really have
anything to say.

A whisper speaks louder than a scream because,
instead of making someone take a step back,
it makes someone take a step forward.

Perhaps time is a drug that helps you heal.
But I'll have OD'd by then.

시간이 약이라는데
도대체 몇 알을
먹어야 하나?

Cartoonist Lee Mal Nyun's handwriting

만화가 **이말년**의 손글씨

It was too shallow of a love
for me to fall in.

Yes,
years later when we look back,
this moment may be an insignificant dot in time.

But whether or not this dot
was the starting point of a rising line or a falling one
will be significant.

163

This too
should not
pass.

No worry can stand taller
than a friend who worries with you.

166

You have a better chance of trying your best
once you realize that it's best to try.

Breathing
is the art of embodying the sky.

At times,
maybe is all that you may be.

The truth
doesn't require acknowledgement
to be exactly what it is.

Means nothing to me to be called a good man
by a world of bad men.

Not
loving
yourself
back
is also

unrequited
love.

172

Whenever I'm told to thank the heavens,
I happen to be looking down at the ground.

Trying not to do things you'll be sorry for is love,
but to be sorry is also love.

173

What do I do when
where I want to go,
where I have to go,
and where I'm going
never converge?

Cry, but never weep.
Fall, but never collapse.

My photo ID
appears to be identifying how ugly I am.

Even if my phone was the one using me,
it wouldn't make me smart.

Perhaps we're living in a world where
ignorant and relatable,
crude and honest,
have become perfectly interchangeable.

The people responsible for your savings
apparently aren't responsible for your saving.

180

Good lyrics
make you feel
that this song was loved.

You made me fall *in* love,
so you have to help me out.

Designer Kimm Kijo's handwriting

디자이너 **김기조**의 손글씨

Swiped and unlocked.

184

The antique aficionado
wanted to be forever young.

If you envy the gifted,
try opening the gift in your hands.

186

The person who pushed you to the edge
is preferable
to the person who tips you off of it.

If you own things but cherish nothing,
it doesn't make you wealthy,
it makes you a garbage can.

I had a wonderful song playing loud.
There was a noise complaint.

Soundproofing won't be enough for the tasteproof.

People in your way
are probably just as lost as you.

Some things can only be seen
with your eyes shut
and your heart open.

Now that I've let go,
I see some things worth holding on to.

"I did it wrong"
isn't the same as
"I did wrong."

It's all right.

Failure is just my B-roll.

Someone that comes to mind on cold days
isn't necessarily a warm person.

Be careful
not to mistake a hangover
for regret.

Loving you
is like blocking a train with my body.

I reminisce,
not to dwell in the past,
but to practice for a future worth remembering.

198

He just wouldn't leave me alone.
He's doing it even now,
by leaving me alone.

Allow me
just one thing
that is
mine.

200

There are no vacancies in my mind
but I'm the only guest without a room.

You don't have to know everything
but not knowing everything certainly doesn't help.

Don't throw me a bone
if it requires me to work like a dog.

Try telling a cow
that it's no use crying over spilled milk.

There's a fine line between a lovers' quarrel and lovers of quarrels.

They say there's a time and place for everything,
but I have neither a watch nor a map.

"You're the greatest gift of all!"

Wait till you see me unwrapped.

You'll do.
No need for the whole world.

A worm can fly
only in the beak of a bird.

People who say they'll choose to be themselves
even if they were born again,
are either hard workers or slackers.

Passion
is the narrowing of the gap between
who I wish to be
and who I will be.

Student Lee Seo Rim's handwriting

학생 이서림의 손글씨

As a kid, there was so much I didn't want to hear.

Now that I'm older,
I'd die to hear some of those things.

The duet that gave birth to me
is full of discord
but it sounds just fine to my ears.

I'm not lazy.
I'm just busy being lazy.

If there was an "Ignore" button next to the "Like" button, would you even see it?

Lovers meet over coffee
and break up over coffee.

Coffee is the official drink of hope and heartbreak.

My heart
goes through four seasons in a single day.

What is clearly struggle
looks like flapping of the wings to me.

The depth of someone
can only be realized
once you swim out of them.

Two halves
only make a hole.

Parents.

Next time you wish you got to choose them,
remember that they also didn't choose you.

A true waste of time
is not using time even as a waste.

Spring.

The way my year is jumping off, it appears to be broken.

I wrote a note to not forget
but I forgot where the note is.

That's what's happened between us.

The burden of having to look at the big picture
is only making me step back.

I said to a friend, "Good luck,"
and he responded,
"You think luck is gonna do the work for me?"

We need
a new
emotion
that is
apathy
and
sympathy
at the same
time.

228

You passed me by without a word,
hand in hand with someone else.

The words that came to mind:
factory reset.

The hammer that drove a nail through your heart
is the very thing that can pull it out.

"Are you sure you want to delete?"

There are things that will be saved no matter how
many times you click "OK."

The fact
that you
don't feel
any guilt

doesn't
make you
any less
guilty.

231

232

The architecture of memories:

constructed by the mind,
renovated by the heart.

Sometimes regret
is just a sign
of a healthy imagination.

Surely, there must have been a moment between us
when even this dullness
was something new and exciting.

What you need to hear more from yourself is not
"Yes you can,"
but "Yes you may."

236

Live each day as if it is your last.

This day will most certainly be the last time being this day.

Love that begins from afar
should never end up close.

238

Each time I tear off a page of the calendar,
it feels like a page of me is being ripped away with it.

If you must cry,
at least don't do it alone.

With
the strength
you've mustered
to hold on
to the things
you're losing,

grab ahold
of yourself.

I'd like to be able to line your way back home
with a red carpet.

Radio DJ Bae Chul Soo's handwriting

라디오 DJ 배 철수의 손글씨

I wish life was a playlist,
so that I can slip in a happy song
behind all of these sad ones.

인생이 플레이리스트 같았으면 좋겠다.
슬픈 노래 뒤에
밝은 노래 하나 준비해두게.

Sometimes I miss missing you.

Maybe the halves we left behind to become one
would have made a better one.

I'm telling you not to worry,
not because it's something that won't happen,
but because it's something that mustn't.

You're looking for someone who will listen,
and that someone is looking for something to hear.

If you grow too close, the breakup
will be that much harder.

This is my relationship with the world.

The person I miss most
happens to be me.

250

Nothing is forever.
I pray that this truth isn't either.

A day
too beautiful

to only be
remembered.

When I no longer have the strength to
hold up an umbrella for you,
I'll stand with you in the rain.

타블로의 손글씨

Sweet dreams.

좋은 꿈 꾸세요

BLONOTE

초판 1쇄 인쇄 2016년 12월 14일
초판 1쇄 발행 2016년 12월 21일

지은이　　타블로

편집장　　김지향
편집　　　이희숙 박선주 김지향
모니터링　김지영
디자인　　최정윤
제작　　　강신은 김동욱 임현식
마케팅　　방미연 이재익
홍보　　　김희숙 김상만 이천희

펴낸이　　이병률
펴낸곳　　달 출판사
출판등록　2009년 5월 26일 제406-2009-000034호
주소　　　10881 경기도 파주시 회동길 210
전자우편　dal@munhak.com
페이스북　/dalpublishers
트위터　　@dalpublishers
인스타그램　dalpublishers
전화번호　031-955-1921(편집) 031-955-2688(마케팅)
팩스　　　031-955-8855
ISBN　　　979-11-5816-051-7 03810

● 이 도서의 국립중앙도서관 출판예정도서목록(CIP)은 서지정보유통지원시스템
홈페이지(http://seoji.nl.go.kr)와 국가자료공동목록시스템(http://www.nl.go.kr/kolisnet)에서
이용하실 수 있습니다. (CIP제어번호 : CIP2016029598)